D0126469

# THE CHRISTMAS TUGBOAT

## HOW THE ROCKEFELLER CENTER CHRISTMAS TREE
## CAME TO NEW YORK CITY

CALGARY PUBLIC LIBRARY

DEC 2012

by **George Matteson** and **Adele Ursone**   Paintings by **James E. Ransome**

Clarion Books • Houghton Mifflin Harcourt
Boston   New York   2012

Clarion Books • 215 Park Avenue South, New York, New York 10003 • Text copyright © 2012 by George Matteson and Adele Ursone • Illustrations
copyright © 2012 by James E. Ransome • All rights reserved. • For information about permission to reproduce selections from this book, write to
Permissions, Houghton Mifflin Harcourt Publishing Company, 215 Park Avenue South, New York, New York 10003. • Clarion Books is an imprint
of Houghton Mifflin Harcourt Publishing Company. • www.hmhbooks.com • The text was set in Arlt. • Title hand-lettering by Kelly Hume • The
illustrations were executed in acrylics. • Library of Congress Cataloging-in-Publication Data • Matteson, George, 1948– • The Christmas tugboat : how
the Rockefeller Center Christmas tree came to New York City / by George Matteson and Adele Ursone ; illustrated by James E. Ransome. • p. cm.
Summary: A New York Harbor tugboat captain and his family take the tug up the Hudson River to pick up and tow the barge carrying the enormous
Christmas tree that will be displayed at Rockefeller Center. • ISBN 978-0-618-99215-7 (hardcover) • [1. Tugboats—Fiction. 2. Boats and
boating—Fiction. 3. Family life—New York—Fiction. 4. Christmas trees—Fiction. 5. Hudson River Valley (N.Y. and N.J.)—Fiction. 6. New York
(State)—Fiction.] I. Ursone, Adele. II. Ransome, James E., ill. III. Title. • PZ7.M43166Chr 2012 • [Fic]—dc23 • 2011041795
Manufactured in China • SCP   10   9   8   7   6   5   4   3   2   1
4500363423

For Emily.
For all who bring joy.
—G.M. & A.U.


For the inspiring words of
George Matteson and Adele Ursone.
—J.E.R.

SOMETIMES IN THE MIDDLE OF THE NIGHT, I wake to the ringing of my dad's alarm clock. Lying still, I listen to the familiar sounds from my parents' room as Dad puts on the clothes he laid out the night before. He likes to dress and get out of the house quickly so he doesn't disturb Mom and me. My dad is a New York Harbor tugboat captain. He goes to work at all times of the day and night, depending on the tides, the weather, what he's towing, and where he's towing it.

This morning is different. When I hear the alarm, I jump out of bed and hurry into my clothes. Mom does the same, and in no time the three of us are out of the house. The streets are dark, and the winter air on my face is chilly. I think of my friends still asleep, curled up in their warm beds, while I'm leaving on a special job. Dad, Mom, and I will be gone two days. We're taking the tug up the Hudson River and bringing back a giant Christmas tree for Rockefeller Center in New York City!

We drive to the waterfront and park next to the creepy old Brooklyn pier, where the tugboat is docked. As we walk onto the pier, shadows dart out at us from the piles of junk and lumber all around.

I move closer to Dad. But as my eyes adjust to the darkness, I see that it's only the cats that live at the pier, gathering around to see if we've brought them some food. "Sorry, cats. No time to stop and play with you now," I tell them. "We've got work to do."

Mom and I follow Dad very carefully as he steps onto a barge tied along the dock. Then, one after the other, we take his hand and hop down onto the big rubber bow fender of the tug, then onto the deck itself. Mom, as always, watches me closely. She worries I might fall in the water, but Dad knows I'll be okay. He's taught me the most important lesson of a boatman: Pay attention!

Our first job is to start the engine. Dad and I go down the steep stairs into the engine room while Mom sorts out the lines on deck. The air down here feels even colder than outside. The room is brightly lit, with different-colored pipes and wires running all around. Right in the middle, standing all alone, is the engine. It's about a hundred times bigger than I am and painted shiny yellow.

Dad shows me how to check it out before we start. "Oil, water, and diesel fuel. That's all it takes to make an engine happy," he tells me.

"Okay, put your hands over your ears," he warns, and he puts on earmuffs to protect himself from the sound. As he pushes the starter button next to the engine, there's the loudest noise I've ever heard. Even with Dad's warning, I still jump! The whole boat shivers as the engine starts. Then the sound quickly evens out and drops to a deep rumble. Dad signals for both of us to go on deck. I keep my hands over my ears until I'm back outside.

With the engine warm, we're ready to go. Mom and Dad cast off our lines. Then she and I coil them on deck while he steps into the pilothouse, the place you go to steer and navigate the boat. Dad says that the engine room is where you keep the horsepower, but the pilothouse is where you keep the brainpower.

Dad backs the tug away from the pier, turns upriver, and shifts ahead. In front of us, the tall glass buildings of Lower Manhattan catch the gray dawn. They look as if they're sleeping. Off to the left is the Statue of Liberty. Her torch is lit, and she looks wide awake. As we steer around the tip of Manhattan and head north, up the Hudson River, the sun comes up, winking on and off between the skyscrapers as we pass. I press my nose against the pilothouse window, feeling the sun's warmth through the glass.

Below deck, up in the bow, is the place where the crew lives while the boat is out working. You get to it by going down a stairway from the pilothouse. There's a little kitchen, a dining table, a bathroom, and a couple of bunk beds. It's cozy, like a big doll house. I go down to the kitchen to help Mom make oatmeal for breakfast. Then we carry the steaming bowls up so we can all eat in the pilothouse.

You get used to things moving slowly when you're on a tug. The fastest we'll go, even when the current is with us, is about nine knots. That's like driving your car eleven miles an hour. Pretty slow! But I love watching the river go by and listening to Dad tell stories passed down to him by some of the older captains he's worked with—stories about storms and pirates and explosions at sea.

On a boat it can get kind of boring if you aren't doing something like telling stories. Whenever I go, I bring paints and lots of paper. I try to paint some of the things I see, like the sun shining between the skyscrapers. Other times, I help with chores like polishing the brass in the pilothouse. But my favorite thing to do is steer the boat.

When I first learned how to do it—when I was really little—I wasn't very good. I'd turn the steering wheel too far one way and then too far the other way, making the boat zigzag. Dad used to say that when I steered, the boat's track through the water looked like a big snake slithering from side to side. But now I can keep a pretty steady course, and he says it looks like we're sailing straight down Broadway.

If I sit in the captain's chair I'm not tall enough to see ahead, so I kneel in it instead. Dad stands beside me, holding a chart of the river. He points out how the chart shows things we see around us: Red buoys marking one side of the channel and green buoys marking the other. Rocks, lighthouses, and docks. Telephone cables and pipelines that cross under the river. There are even marks that tell you what the mud on the bottom is like.

We travel upriver most of the day. Finally, just as the sun is getting low, we near Stony Point, where we'll pick up our tow. Suddenly, I let out a yell. Ahead, tied up along the shore, is a big black barge. It's much bigger than our boat, and it's decorated with huge—I mean *huge*—red Christmas ornaments. Riding on the deck of the barge is a full-size tractor trailer truck. And lying down on the truck bed is the tree. It's all bound up with rope, just like the Christmas trees we've carried home. But it's twenty times as big!

Dad drifts the tug into shallow water next to the barge. There is a crowd of people standing there waiting for us, so he climbs up to talk to them and make sure everything is tied down securely. We wouldn't want to lose an ornament—let alone the whole truck—overboard.

In just a few minutes, Dad is back on the tugboat, fixing the towline. The people who were on the barge climb back on shore, and we're ready to go. Then everything seems to happen in slow motion. Dad nudges the tug ahead until the towline just comes tight, and the barge swings around right behind us and begins to follow us back down the river toward the city.

"We'll tow a few hours and then tie up for the night at an abandoned pier I know," Dad says. "We'll go the rest of the way in the morning."

Happy
RO

21

A half moon glows high in the sky. Stars begin to appear around it, and a cold wind rises with the darkness. The water is black, and the pinpoints of light on shore are so bright, they seem to be set right in the pilothouse windows.

How can Dad see where to go? It gets darker and darker in the pilothouse, and I wish we could turn on the lights. But Dad says you mustn't do that when you're running at night. Your eyes have to adjust to the dark. If you turn on a light, your eyes lose their night vision. Then, when you turn it off, they have to get used to the dark all over again, and that can take a long time.

Dad takes me on his lap, and I feel warm and safe as he points out the marks he's steering by—the small lights of the buoys blinking red and green, the beacon lights on shore. "For tugboats, night is the same as day —only darker," he says with a chuckle.

Mom comes up to tell us dinner is ready. I go down below to eat with her while Dad eats in the pilothouse and steers. It's chicken and rice, and I finish every bite on my plate.

By the time we reach the abandoned pier, the wind is blowing so hard, I can hear it whistle. Will we be able to get the barge to the dock safely? I can't see a thing except the huge black shape of the barge looming behind the tug, and it is *not* a comforting sight!

"Don't worry," Dad calls. "The wind is perfect. Docking this thing won't be a problem."

Very carefully, he brings us in close. Then he lets the wind gently push us up against the pier, where we'll rest for the night.

Dad steps out on deck, picks up a line, and throws it around one of the mooring posts on the dock. Then Mom climbs up and walks back to tie up the barge, which is lying quietly behind us, the wind holding it in place.

"Simple as that!" says Dad as he clicks on the lights in the pilothouse.

"Easy for you to say," answers Mom. And we all grin as we squint our eyes against the bright light.

In no time the engine is shut down and everything is set for the night. The only thing left on is the generator that will give us electricity for lights and heat. When we're in our bunks, I ask Mom if she'll sing the barges song for me. It was one of the first ones she taught me, and I love the words.

*Out of my window, looking in the night,*
*I can see the barges' flickering light.*
*Silently flows the river to the sea,*
*and the barges, too, go silently.*

The roar of the engine startles me awake. Mom and I both sit up in surprise.

"Morning! Everybody up," calls Dad.

I hop out of bed and get dressed. Even as Mom and I climb the stairs to the pilothouse, Dad is steering the tug and barge away from the dock, setting off downriver again.

The sun isn't up yet. Only the first pink glow of dawn is spreading through the sky. But I can see that a thick coat of frost has settled on the tug and everything on shore.

As the first sunlight brushes across the land, Mom points back to the tree. It sparkles all over as if covered with tiny diamonds. "The night and the cold have decorated it just for us," she says.

py Holidays
OCKEFELLER
CENTER

It's fully daylight as we approach the George Washington Bridge. Suddenly, a helicopter roars overhead and hovers right above us. Then another is flying around us, and another. With my heart pounding, I race on deck. The helicopters are from the New York City TV stations, and they're taking pictures of us for the morning news. I didn't realize anyone knew we were coming! They circle us again and again, so close I can feel whooshes of air from their blades. I wave to them, wondering if Grandma and Grandpa and my friends are watching us on TV.

A little farther downriver, two bright blue police boats arrive and take up positions on either side of our bow. Then a tour boat crowded with school kids comes out from the shore to greet us.

In a minute we'll swing past the Statue of Liberty and around the Battery, the very tip of Manhattan. Dad gets up from his seat. He gestures for me to take his place in front of the helm. "Here. I think you should steer for a little bit," he says. "Don't worry, I'll be right beside you."

I am towing the Christmas tree through the very middle of New York Harbor! A big red and white fireboat pulls alongside. I wonder if there's a fire nearby—if the tree might be on fire. But the firemen march out on deck in their blue uniforms and point their huge fire nozzles straight up at the sky. Then with a rush of sound, jets of red, white, and blue water flash into the air above us.

"Steady as you go," Dad says quietly, and I hold the very best course I can as I steer through the colorful mist.

Dad takes back the wheel to land the tug and barge along the seawall in the East River, just under the Manhattan Bridge. As soon as we're tied up, workers rush onto the barge to get the truck and the tree ready to go ashore. By tomorrow morning it has to be set up in midtown, standing tall and unbound, ready for its lights and decorations—and visitors. There's no time to waste, and everyone is in a hurry.

Mom helps me onto the barge to get my first close-up look at the tree. Touching one of its branches and smelling that wonderful Christmas smell, I feel sad that our part of the adventure is over.

Just then, one of the workers kneels beside me. "Would you like me to find you a souvenir?" he whispers.

"Yes, please!" I whisper back. I watch as he pokes around among the tree's topmost branches. He finds something and brings it to me.

It's a perfect little pinecone, brown and rough. It nestles in my hand as if it's alive. When it opens up, I'll plant the seeds. Then maybe someday we'll have a New York City Christmas tree right in our own backyard.

# About This Book

For two hundred years tugboats have done just about every job on the water that you can imagine. They've helped move ships in and out of harbors and docking spaces. They've transported big machines that build bridges. They've pulled barges with heating oil, gasoline, coal, bricks, lumber, and most everything else that keeps our country moving and growing. For the tugboat's crew, the work is often monotonous, sometimes dangerous, and always requires careful attention and long hours in all sorts of weather.

For many years, I was captain of a tugboat that did all the usual tasks. Then, late one November, I got the assignment to fetch the towering Rockefeller Center Christmas tree and bring it by barge down the Hudson River to New York City. It was not a difficult job, so it seemed a good opportunity to bring my wife, Adele, and our young daughter along.

Much later, Adele realized that the adventure was ideal for a children's book. So we proceeded to write our story, handing the manuscript back and forth and sharing it with our daughter along the way.

Through the years there have been many interesting tales surrounding the Rockefeller Center Christmas trees and their travels to midtown Manhattan. We are pleased to share the story of our very special voyage.

GEORGE MATTESON


Almost twenty years ago, my wife and I moved to New York's Hudson Valley, with dreams of sailing on the river and walking along its banks. Although we rarely have time for those things, the river still brings me great joy whenever I find myself next to it.

One of my greatest pleasures is riding the train south to New York City or north to Syracuse, where I teach. It's wonderful to gaze out the window and survey the Hudson in all its moods. Often on my train rides I'll see a tugboat, its diminutive size giving little hint of the strength it possesses as it pushes or pulls heavy loads up- or downriver. I always wonder where it's going and what type of cargo it's tugging—and then my train will go around a bend, or a group of trees will cut off the view. So it was a joy to spend uninterrupted hours with the tug in this story.

I like to challenge myself to use a different palette for each book that I illustrate. For *The Christmas Tugboat* I wanted to capture both the chill of winter and the warm and cozy feeling of the family working together. I used bright red and white for the tugboat, so it would stand out against the neutral waters and skyline. I also studied photos of the tug's journey and used models to stand in for the original family. I hope you enjoy reading this book as much as I enjoyed creating the illustrations for it.

JAMES E. RANSOME